This AR test dedicated in honor of
Teacher Debbie
From Ryan Peters
MTS 2005

To my parents, Louis and Judith Mammano,

with love and appreciation which goes beyond words.

Typeset in Gill Sans Ultra

Printed in Hong Kong.

Library of Congress Cataloging in Publication Data.

Rhinos who surf / Julie Mammano.

Summary: Rhinos who surf get up early, paddle out, and have fun

until the sun goes down when they ride the last wave to shore.

Includes surfer lingo and a glossary of terms.

ISBN: 0-8118-1000-3 (hc)

[1. Surfing—Fiction. 2. Rhinoceroses—Fiction.] I. Title.

PZ7.M3117Rh 1996 95-38240

[E]—dc20 CIP

AC

Distributed in Canada by Raincoast Books

8680 Cambie Street, Vancouver, B.C. V6P 6M9

Distributed in Australia and

New Zealand by CIS•Cardigan Street

245-249 Cardigan Street, Carlton 3053 Australia

10 9 8 7 6 5 4 3 2

Chronicle Books, 85 Second Street

San Francisco, California 94105

Rhinos Who Surf

BY JULIE MAMMANO

chronicle books

SAN FRANCISCO

Rhinos who surf
get up early.

They grab their **BOARDS...**

. . . and hop in the car.
WE SRF

As they JAM
to the beach,
they scrounge
for quarters
to feed
the meter.
TIDE CHART
GUM
DRIVER LICENSE
1¢

Surf All Day
2
4
6
8
25¢

The waves are MAJOR HUGE and FULLY PUMPING!

They WAX their boards.

They PADDLE out.

Rhinos who surf have no fear of **MONDO** waves.

They **SHRED!**
They **DROP IN!**

They CARVE UP THE FACE.

They GO VERTICAL
and SLAM THE LIP.

They pull **KILLER AERIALS.**

When they SHOOT THE TUBE,
they are WAY COOL in
the GREEN ROOM.

Rhinos who
surf have
FULL-ON
GNARLY
WIPE-OUTS.

They are **PITCHED** over the **FALLS.**

They are **LAUNCHED** through the air.

They are THRASHED in the RINSE CYCLE below.

They are forced to BAIL
on some TASTY RIDES
when DWEEBS
SNAKE their waves.

They surf until the
sun goes down
then they ride
the last wave to shore.

They are
TOTALLY AMPED!

Rhinos who surf are WAY tired

and dream about another day of
EXCELLENT and
AWESOME surf.

Surf Lingo

Aerial a surfing move done in the air

Amped really happy

Awesome great

Bail jump off a surfboard to avoid an accident

Boards surfboards

Carve up do lots of skillful moves on a wave

Cool really good

Drop in slide from the top of a wave to the bottom

Dweebs jerks who surf

Excellent great

Face the big blue part of the wave

Falls the crashing part of a wave that forms a waterfall

Full-on very

Fully very

Go vertical make a sharp upward movement on a wave

Gnarly bad, scary

Green room the space inside a tube wave

Jam go really fast

Killer really great

Launched be thrown in the air (usually from a *gnarly wipe out*)

Major very

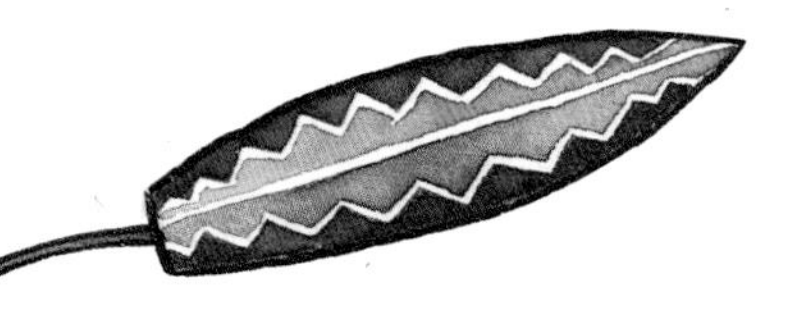

Mondo very big

Paddle move your arms through the water, like an oar, to propel the surfboard

Pitched be thrown in the air

Pumping (waves) coming in one after another

Rinse cycle the choppy, churning water from a crashing wave

Shoot the tube surf through the tube

Shred surf really well

Slam the lip hit the top of a wave as it starts to curl over

Snake steal someone else's wave

Tasty really great

Thrashed get tumbled around in the water

Totally very

Tube a wave that forms a tube or pipe shape

Wax sticky stuff that makes a surfer's feet stay on the board

Way very

Wipe-out a fall or a crash

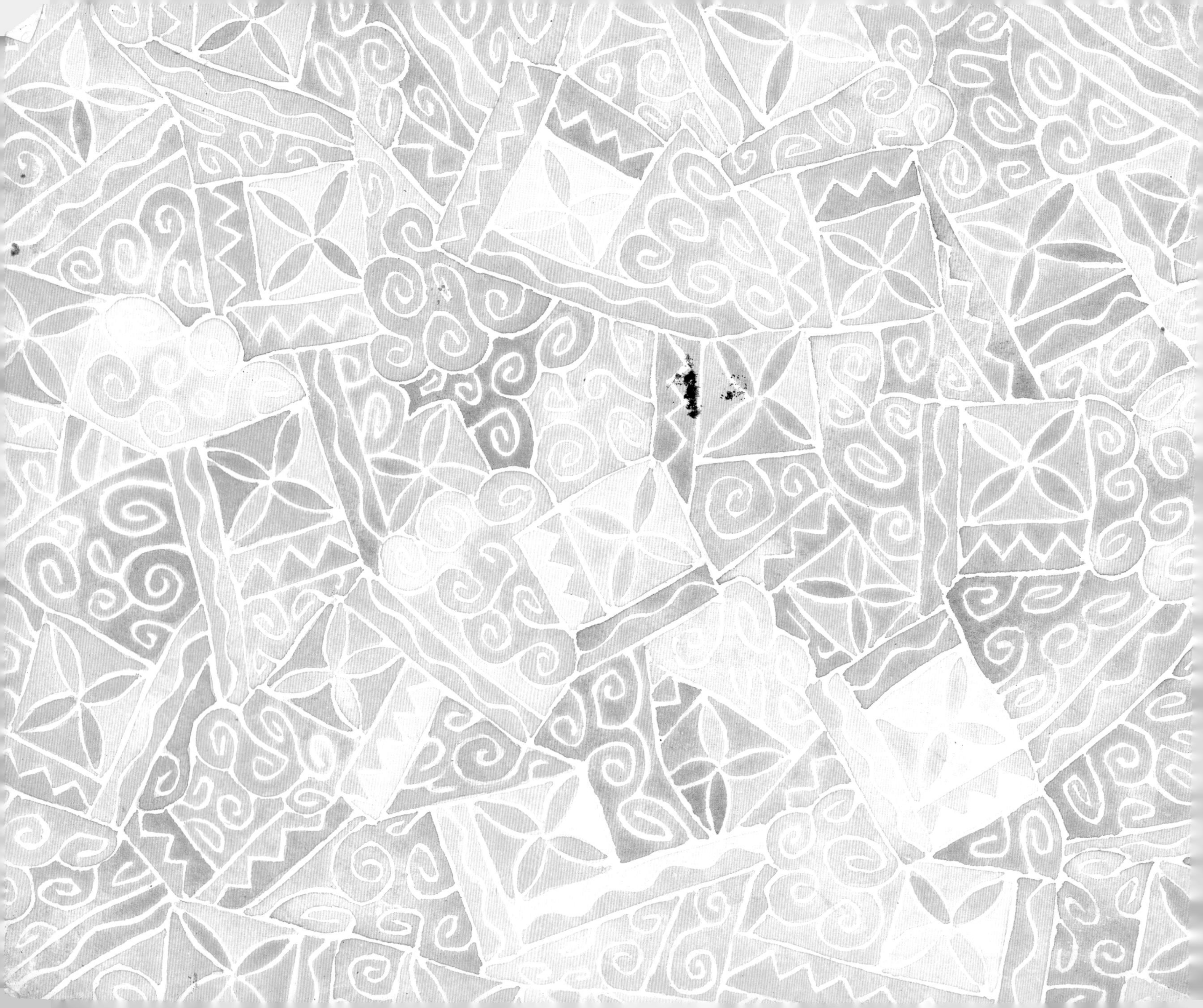